To Henrietta Smith,
Effie Lee Morris, and inspired
librarians whose outreach
takes us all in.

Let it Shine

Atheneum Books for Young Readers * An imprint of Simon & Schuster Children's Publishing Division *
1230 Avenue of the Americas * New York, New York 10020 * Copyright © 2007 by Ashley Bryan *
All rights reserved, including the right of reproduction in whole or in part in any form. * Book design by Ann
Bobco * The text of this book is set in Tiepolo. * The illustrations are rendered with construction paper. *
Manufactured in China * 10 9 8 7 6 5 4 3 2   * Library of Congress Cataloging-in-Publication
Data * Let it shine: three favorite spirituals / [illustrated by] Ashley Bryan. — 1st ed. * p.   cm. * Summary:
Illustrated versions of three well-known hymns. * ISBN-13: 978-0-689-84732-5 * ISBN-10: 0-689-84732-7 *
1. Hymns, English—Juvenile literature. [1. Hymns. 2. Spirituals (Songs)] I. Bryan, Ashley, ill. II. This little
light of mine. III. When the saints go marching in. IV. He's got the whole world in His hands. V. Title.
BV353 .S68 2007 * 782.25'3'0268—dc22 * 2003012028

Atheneum Books for Young Readers New York London Toronto Sydney

Let it Shine

three favorite spirituals

ASHLEY BRYAN

This Little Light of Mine

This little light of mine, I'm gonna let it shine.
This little light of mine, I'm gonna let it shine.

This little light of mine, I'm gonna let it shine.
Let it shine, let it shine, let it shine.

Hide it under a bushel? (No!) I'm gonna let it shine.
Hide it under a bushel? (No!) I'm gonna let it shine.

Hide it under a bushel? (No!) I'm gonna let it shine.
Let it shine, let it shine, let it shine.

Don't let Satan blow it out, I'm gonna let it shine.
Don't let Satan blow it out, I'm gonna let it shine.

Don't let Satan blow it out, I'm gonna let it shine.
Let it shine, let it shine, let it shine.

Ev'ry where I go, I'm gonna let it shine.
Ev'ry where I go, I'm gonna let it shine.

Ev'ry where I go, I'm gonna let it shine.
Let it shine, let it shine, let it shine.

Oh, When the Saints Go Marching in

Oh, when the saints go marching in,
Oh, when the saints go marching in,

Oh, Lord I want to be in that number,
when the saints go marching in.

Oh, when the sun refuse to shine,
Oh, when the sun refuse to shine,

Oh, Lord I want to be in that number,
when the sun refuse to shine.

Oh, when the stars have disappeared,
Oh, when the stars have disappeared,

Oh, Lord I want to be in that number,
when the stars have disappeared.

Oh, when they crown Him Lord of Lords
Oh, when they crown Him Lord of Lords,

Oh, Lord I want to be in that number,
When they crown Him Lord of Lords.

Oh, when the children play in peace,
Oh, when the children play in peace,

Oh, Lord I want to be in that number,
when the children play in peace.

He's got the whole world in His hands,
He's got the whole world in His hands,

He's got the whole world in His hands,
He's got the whole world in His hands.

He's got the sun and the moon in His hands,
He's got the wind and the rain in His hands,

He's got the stars in the sky in His hands,
He's got the whole world in His hands.

He's got the rivers and the seas in His hands,
He's got the flowers and the trees in His hands,

He's got the mountains and the valleys in His hands,
He's got the whole world in His hands.

He's got the lion and the lamb in His hands,
He's got the tiger and the ram in His hands,

He's got the sparrow and the dove in His hands,
He's got the whole world in His hands.

He's got the little bitty baby in His hands,
He's got the little bitty baby in His hands,

He's got the little bitty baby in His hands,
He's got the whole world in His hands,

He's got you and me, brother, in His hands,
He's got you and me, sister, in His hands,

He's got everybody in His hands,
He's got the whole world in His hands.

THIS LITTLE LIGHT

This lit—tle light of mine,   I'm gon-na let it   shine.
Hide it under a bushel? (No!)   I'm gon-na let it   shine.
Don't let Satan blow it   out,   I'm gon-na let it   shine.
Ev — 'ry   where I go,   I'm gon-na let it   shine.

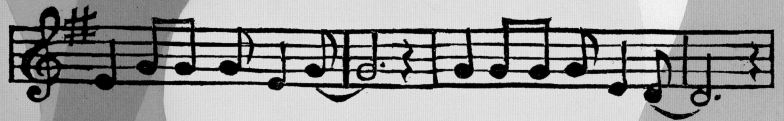

This lit—tle light of mine,   I'm gon-na let it   shine.
Hide it under a bushel? (No!)   I'm gon-na let it   shine.
Don't let Satan blow it   out,   I'm gon-na let it   shine.
Ev — 'ry   where I go,   I'm gon-na let it   shine.

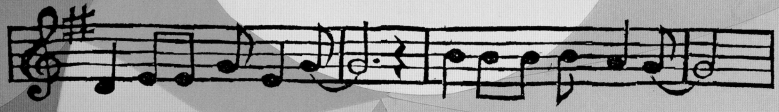

This lit—tle light of mine,   I'm gon-na let it   shine.
Hide it under a bushel? (No!)   I'm gon-na let it   shine.
Don't let Satan blow it   out,   I'm gon-na let it   shine.
Ev — 'ry   where I go,   I'm gon-na let it   shine.

Let it shine, let it shine,   let it shine.

WHEN THE SAINTS

Oh, when the saints go march-ing in, Oh, when the
Oh, when the sun re—fuse to shine, Oh, when the
Oh, when the stars have dis—ap — peared, Oh, when the
Oh, when they crown Him Lord of Lords, Oh, when they
Oh, when the child—ren play in peace, Oh, when the

saints go march-ing in, Oh, Lord I want to be in that
sun re — fuse to shine, Oh, Lord I want to be in that
stars have dis- ap — peared, Oh, Lord I want to be in that
crown Him Lord of Lords, Oh, Lord I want to be in that
child–ren play in peace, Oh, Lord I want to be in that

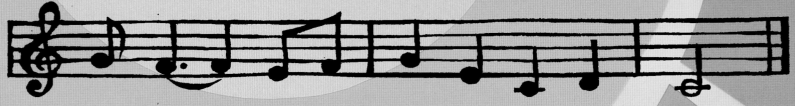

num — ber, when the saints go march-ing in.
num — ber, when the sun re — fuse to shine.
num — ber, when the stars have dis — ap — peared.
num — ber, when they crown Him Lord of Lords.
num — ber, when the child—ren play in peace.

IN HIS HANDS

He's got the whole world in His hands, He's got the
He's got the sun and the moon in His hands, He's got the
He's got the rivers and the seas in His hands, He's got the
He's got the lion and the lamb in His hands, He's got the
He's got the little bitty baby in His hands, He's got the
He's got you and me, brother, in His hands, He's got you

whole world in His hands, He's got the whole world
wind and the rain in His hands, He's got the stars in the sky
flowers and the trees in His hands, He's got the mountains and the valleys
tiger and the ram in His hands, He's got the sparrow and the dove
little bitty baby in His hands, He's got the little bitty baby
and me, sister, in His hands, He's got every — body

in His hands, He's got the whole world in His hands.

Come, let us sing the Spirituals!

The beautiful songs in this book are loved and sung freely throughout the world. Yet they were created by people who were not free—the African-American slaves. The songs were originally called "Negro Spirituals."

It was a crime to teach a slave to read or write. However, the slaves' urges to create could not be bound. In the freedom of the mind, their artistic gifts found expression for their hopes, sorrows, and joys in the creation of the Spiritual. The slaves couldn't write them down, but they could sing them! The Spirituals are unique in the folk songs of the world and are considered one of the finest gifts to world music.

Thousands of these songs have been collected since the end of the Civil War, and have been kept alive by generations of singers. Whether sung by field hands or opera singers, the Spirituals have the power to touch singers and listeners alike.

Throughout the years, many Spirituals have retained their original melodies and verses. Other Spirituals have had verses added or dropped, and melodies have also varied as the spirit moved the singer or the congregation.

I've followed this practice in my offering of *Let it Shine* in an effort to create the most forceful illustrations that will capture the underlying meaning of the Spiritual.

Now let us lift our voices in the celebration of the Spirituals! May the spirit move you to make them your own.